How the Rooster Got His Crown

Retold and illustrated by Amy Lowry Poole

Holiday House / New York

To my daughters—
Logan, Sally, and Nina

This story was adapted from two earlier versions of the tale,
"How the Cock Got His Red Crown," from *The Asian*
Animal Zodiac by Ruth Q. Sun, Rutland, Vermont, &
Tokyo, Japan: Charles Tuttle Company, 1974, and "How the
Cock Got His Red Crown," from *Favorite Children's Stories*
from China and Tibet by Lotta Carswell Hume, Rutland,
Vermont, & Tokyo, Japan: Charles Tuttle Company, 1962.

Copyright © 1999 by Amy Lowry Poole
All Rights Reserved
Printed in the United States of America
First Edition
Design by Sylvia Frezzolini Severance
Library of Congress Cataloging-in-Publication Data
Poole, Amy Lowry.
    How the rooster got his crown
retold and illustrated by Amy Lowry Poole.—1st ed.
    —p. cm.
    Summary: In the early days of the world, when the sun refuses to
come out for fear of a skillful archer's arrows, a small rooster saves the
day by coaxing the sun out with his crowing.
    ISBN 0-8234-1389-6
    [1. Folklore—China.] I. Title.
PZ8.1.P8587Ho 1999
398.2—dc21   98-12311
—[E]   CIP
                                AC

In the western lands of China, the Miao people have lived and farmed the rugged mountains since ancient times. Every evening at dusk, they gather around the village storyteller to hear the legends and history of their people, as the shadows lengthen across the sun-baked courtyard.

Long ago, when the world was new, there was not one but six suns blazing in the sky. The burning heat was relieved every summer by cooling rains. But one year, after the farmers had planted their crops, the rains refused to come, and the heat of the six suns dried up all the tiny seedlings.

At this time Yao was the emperor of China. When he saw the six suns burning up the crops, he was filled with great sorrow, for it meant that his people would starve.

He called for a meeting of the ten wise elders of the village to discuss what could be done to save the harvest.

"We could weave a giant basket and shield the crops from the suns with it," said one.

"Yes, but how will we attach it to the sky?" asked another. They were silent with thought.

After a long pause, the eldest spoke up. "There is only one way. We'll shoot the suns out of the sky with arrows."

The emperor, upon hearing this, immediately sent for the best archers in the kingdom.

On the appointed day, Emperor Yao and the ten wise elders gathered together with the villagers under the burning skies to watch the archers test their skill. With a great burst of energy, the archers shot their arrows high into the sky, only to watch sadly as the arrows fell back onto the parched earth. Time and again they shot in vain at the suns, until the last arrow lay broken upon the ground.

Humiliated, the archers bowed low before the emperor.

"Our arrows cannot reach the suns for they are too far away."

Once again the emperor summoned the elders to a meeting.

"We must act quickly or our people will starve," he said.

The eldest spoke up. "Why not ask Prince Haoyi from the land beyond the mountains to help us? He is said to be very clever, and his skill as an archer is known throughout China."

So Emperor Yao sent his couriers to the green lands beyond the mountains with a message begging the prince to help his people get rid of the suns. The prince agreed and left for the Miao kingdom right away.

Once again the people gathered under the hot skies to see if Prince Haoyi could shoot down the suns. They watched in silence as the prince lifted his mighty bow . . . then slowly laid it down, realizing that his slender arrows would never reach the suns. As he turned to tell the emperor, he noticed the shining suns reflected in a pond and thought to himself, "It will be just the same to shoot them here."

With one strong motion he drew his bow and let loose an arrow into the heart of the first sun, which sank into the bottom of the pond. He fired again and the second sun disappeared. One . . . two . . . three . . . four . . . five times he shot his arrows, and five suns disappeared into the shadows of the pool with a great hissing noise.

When the sixth sun saw what had happened, he became so frightened that he fled from the sky into a cave behind the mountains.

The villagers cheered the mighty prince Haoyi and celebrated with dancing and a feast that lasted until the small hours of the morning. Tired and full of good food and drink, they returned to their mud huts to dream of the upcoming harvest.

When they awoke from their long sleep, they were surprised to find that the sky was still dark. The sun, fearful of Prince Haoyi's mighty arrows, had refused to come out.

The ten wise elders met quickly in the darkness. They begged the sun to come out and shine for them, but he remained in his cave.

"Perhaps our voices aren't strong enough," said one, so they went and brought a tiger to the mouth of the cave.

"ROAR!" went the tiger, but the sun would not come out. The ten wise elders met again. "Perhaps the noise was too loud. Let's try a cow."

So they went and fetched a cow to stand by the cave.

"MOO!" said the cow.

The sun, still frightened, would not come out. The ten wise elders shook their heads, not knowing what to do.

Just then a small rooster, fat with ruffled feathers and a smooth, shiny head, scooted out from one of the huts.

"COCKLE DOODLE DO!" he crowed.

The sun, who was listening, said to himself, "What a lovely sound."

He peeked out over the horizon to see what could be making it. As he slowly came out of his cave, the people began to cheer.

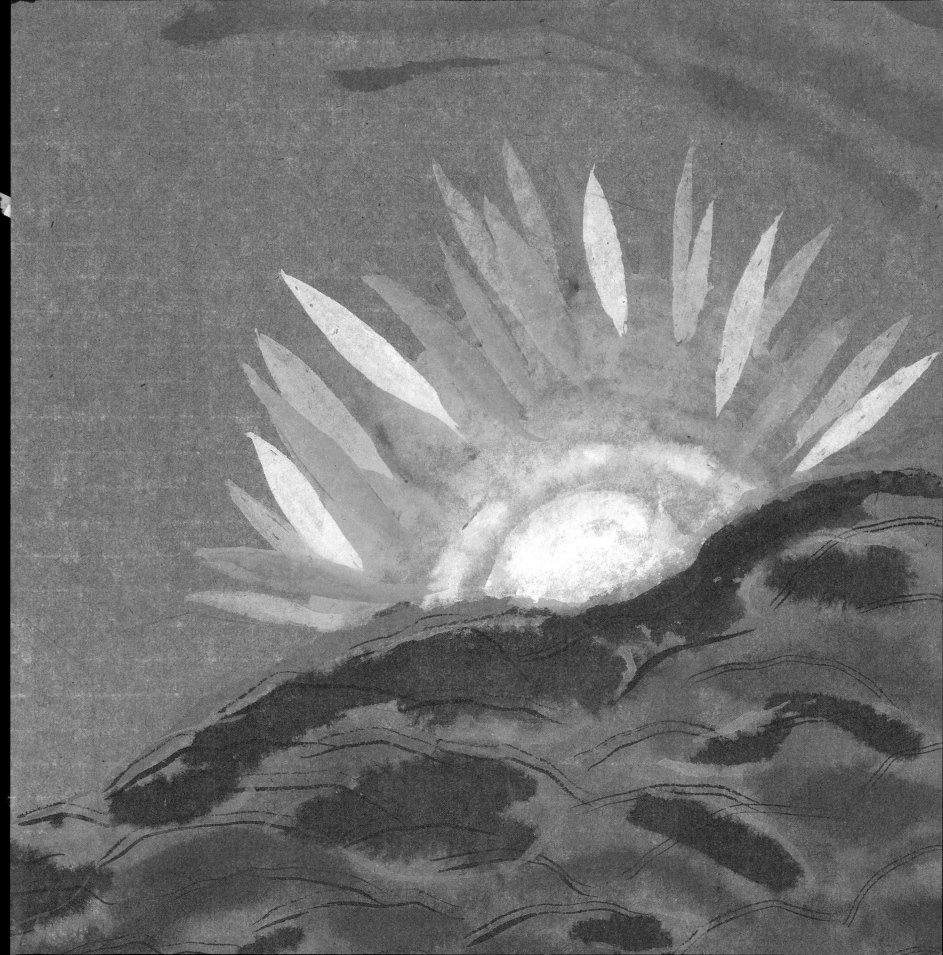

The sixth sun was so pleased that he came out all the way, spreading warmth and light onto the land. When he spied the rooster who had made the sound, he fashioned a small red crown and gently placed it on the rooster's head as thanks.

And to this day, in
the western lands of China,
and all over the world, the
rooster wears a red crown
to call forth the sun.

Author's Note

My daughters and I believe that the five suns who disappeared in the pond under Prince Haoyi's arrows did not in fact die, but returned to earth as important symbols, living on within many ancient traditions.

Shou is the Chinese symbol for long life.

The *spiral* symbolizes the great swirling force of energy, both on earth and in space. In many ancient traditions, it signified the rising of the moon and setting of the sun.

The *yin-yang* circle is one of the primary symbols of Taoist religious beliefs, and represents the two basic conflicting forces of nature. The yin, or dark portion, symbolizes the feminine, as well as the quieter side of nature: earth, water, the night, and the moon. The yang, or white portion, is a masculine symbol, encompassing the day, the sun, the skies, and the heavens. The Taoists believe that true harmony can only be achieved when the two opposites are perfectly balanced. Within the circle of yin-yang, a small seed of the opposite color is contained within each larger shape, signifying their interdependence.

The *raven* is associated with the sun in many different mythologies. The ancient Chinese believed that a three-legged raven lived in the sun, denoting the three phases of the sun: dawn, midday, and dusk. This symbol was countered by that of a frog or toad, who ruled the damp night and lived in the moon.

The *star* takes many forms in folklore. Its meaning frequently depends on its shape, number of points, and arrangement. A five-pointed star often signifies a rising of the spirit. Inverted, it was thought to be a sign of witchcraft. The six-pointed star is most commonly recognized as a symbol of the Judaic religion.

I spent four years in Beijing, China, studying the craft of scroll making and working with Chinese artists. These particular paintings are done on a specially textured rice paper, using Chinese materials of ink and gouache. The paper is then made flat using a traditional method called *Biao Huar*, in which the drawing is mounted onto opaque rice paper using a homemade wheat-based glue.